Alpha-kidZ
Reading Adventures A-Z

Glen Goose
There's A Babysitter On The Loose

Written by Cindy G. Foust
Illustrated by Joyce Revoir

www.AlphakidZ.com

"Glen Goose, There's A Babysitter On The Loose"
is part of the Alpha-kidZ™ series and features one book for each letter A-Z

Written by Cindy G. Foust
Illustrated by Joyce Revoir
Published and distributed by Alpha-kidZ, LLC, West Monroe, Louisiana

Alpha-kidZ is a registered trademark owned by Alpha-kidZ, LLC

First Edition: 2006
Printed in Canada

Second Edition: 2010
Printed in South Korea

ISBN: 978-0-9749220-7-2
UPC: 887556 330023

Read and play online!
www.AlphakidZ.com
email: info@alphakidz.com

To Terry Glen Hamilton
our best friend, our best "Austin"...thanks for believing

1

There is nothing more fun than reading a book in the den, which is exactly what Glen Goose was doing when his father walked in.

2

"As you know, it's Mother's birthday," said Dad, "and I would like to give her a special treat. Would you mind watching the children so we can go out to eat?"

4

5

"Sure! How hard can that be?"
asked Glen. "Everything will be okay.
I am capable of watching
my brother and sister...
you and Mom do it everyday."

6

7

"Grant and Grace,
we are leaving," said Dad.
"I am taking Mom out tonight.
We are leaving Glen in charge,
so please behave...try not to fuss
and fight."

8

After Mom and Dad left for dinner,
Grant and Grace raced down the hall.
"We don't want to stay with you, Glen!
You are no fun at all!"

10

Glen followed his brother and sister where he found them under their bed. "Come out little brother and sister...don't hide. Let's get something to eat instead."

12

13

The little geese dashed
to the kitchen where they
made themselves a snack.
The size of their super-
duper sandwich nearly
gave Glen a heart attack!

"Hey, you can't eat ketchup and jelly beans," said Glen. "That simply will not do. Please sit down at the table and I will cook your dinner for you."

16

After Grant and Grace ate,
Glen began cleaning up their mess.
Suddenly, he heard strange
noises down the hall.
"What was that?" cried Glen.
"I can only guess!"

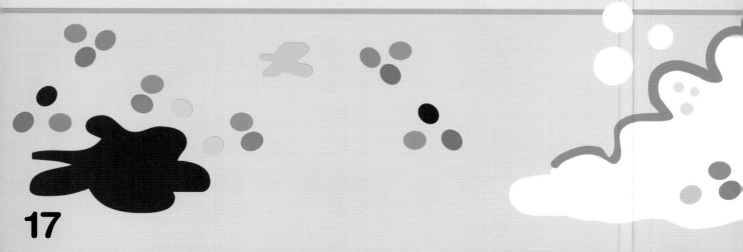

18

19

Glen wasn't sure what
they were doing,
but it was easy to tell,
that whatever it was...
it was a mess, as he followed
the toilet paper trail!

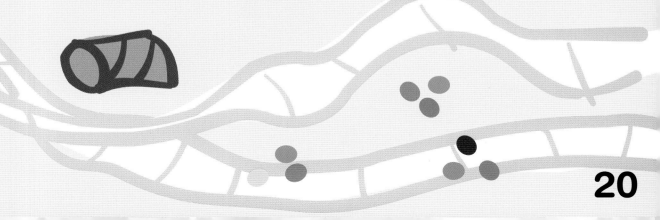

As Glen rounded the corner to the bathroom, it was indeed quite a sight. "Come on in, Glen, the water is fine," said Grace. "We decided to give ourselves a bath tonight!"

23

Glen quickly began mopping
and boy, was the water deep!
"Okay you two, out of the tub!"
he cried. "Go put on your pajamas;
it's time to go to sleep!"

Grant and Grace ignored
their brother and ran to
Mom and Dad's room instead.
Glen found them both jumping...
all wet...in the middle
of their parent's bed!

"Okay you two, time for bed.
I am at the end of my rope.
I wonder if Mom and Dad
will be home soon.
Oh, I can only hope!"

29

Glen passed out in his father's chair, but was unable to take a nap.
"We are so scared,"
cried two little voices.
"Can we climb up in your lap?"

A little later Mom
and Dad came home
as Glen roused up from his chair.
"Hello, everyone. How did it go?"
asked Dad. "Hey, Glen,
what is in your hair?"

"I'm surprised I still have hair!"
exclaimed Glen.
"And I really must confess,
I think it would be easier
to move than to try and
clean up all this mess!"

"I didn't realize being a parent was so hard, and I really admire everything you do. But in case anyone needs me... I'll be in bed, because this place is a zoo!"

The End

Don't End the Fun.
Visit www.AlphakidZ.com

A fun place to learn and play online with interactive books and games.
Shop for Alpha-kidZ books online or find a store near you.

About the Author:
Cindy G. Foust has written a collection of rhyming stories featuring one character and adventure for each letter of the alphabet. She draws inspiration from her family, friends and her own life's experiences. Foust dedicated this book to her brother-in-law, Terry Hamilton, a true friend to Alpha-kidZ. Terry has brought "Austin Alligator" to life, and delighted legions of young fans with his fun and silly antics. In 2003, Foust launched Alpha-kidZ and published her books to celebrate reading and to inspire others. Foust enjoys speaking and reading to children. She lives in her home town of West Monroe, Louisiana with her husband and two children. For more information visit: www.Alphakidz.com.

About the Illustrator:
Joyce Revoir owns a design studio that provides creative solutions for publishing and marketing. She created the bright and vivid signature style for Alpha-kidZ to capture the attention and to stimulate the imagination of young children. Revoir met Foust while attending Louisina Tech University. She resides in Newnan, GA with her husband and two daughters. For more information visit: www.joycerevoir.com.